SAMMY PUFFIN

Book One

PHOTOS BY MICHAEL V. ACOSTA

WRITTEN BY DUANE ZIEGLER

Sammy Puffin Book One

Written by Duane Ziegler
Photography/Illustrations by Michael V. Acosta
Technical Support by Alex Acosta
Edited by Kayla Henley

ISBN: 978-1-7337282-3-2

Library of Congress Control Number: 2019905262

Published by Duane Ziegler

Light of the Moon, Inc. - Publishing Division
Book Design/Production/Consulting
Carbondale, Colorado
www.lightofthemooninc.com

This book is dedicated to
Michael and Alex Acosta,
who spent two weeks in Newfoundland
visiting Alex's favorite animal, puffins.

Michael photographed puffins and other wildlife
and contributed illustrated versions
of those photos to the Sammy books.

"Sammy, open your mouth
and I will feed you,"
Daddy Puffin coaxed.

Mommy Puffin laughed.
"Sammy, now it is my
turn to feed you."

Sammy Puffin was hungry
and opened his mouth very wide.
Feeding time was easy for
Sammy because he
was always hungry.

Mommy said, "Today we will have swimming lessons. Please swim with me. First, we swim in a circle, then we swim in a straight line, and then we swim again in a circle. Great job, Sammy!"

Daddy then said,
"Sammy, while you swim,
dive like this and see if you
can catch some fish."

Sammy followed his
daddy into the water.
Sammy dove and came up
with his mouth full of fish!

13

"Sammy, it is time to practice wing exercises," Mommy declared. "We will count one, one. Then two, two. And then three, three."

Sammy moved his wings so fast
that he lifted off the ground!
"Whoa!" Sammy shouted,
and almost tipped over.

"Sammy, spread your wings out and walk in a circle," Mommy coached. "Now walk quickly. Now run fast. Run a little faster, then jump into the air. Beat your wings very hard. Great job, Sammy; you are flying!"

Sammy smiled and smiled
as he flew around and
landed back on the ground.

"I love Mommy and Daddy.
I am happy to be a puffin.
It is so much fun!"

ABOUT THE AUTHOR

Duane Ziegler was raised on a farm in North Dakota with five brothers. While he had a strong attraction to the wheat fields, pasture land, and rolling prairies, the mountains of Colorado have been the biggest influence in his life. He has been a professional educator for twenty years and a professional real estate agent for twenty-three years. He is a member of SCBWI, Colorado Authors League, and Roaring Fork Writers' Group. His immediate family includes his wife Sandy, two children DeAnn and Nathan, and three grandchildren. He thanks the many people supporting him in creating children's fiction.

Visit Duane's Website duaneziegler.com
Or connect with him on Facebook @duanezieglerauthor

ABOUT THE PHOTOGRAPHER

Michael Acosta is an avid photographer who loves to take photos of beautiful and rare wildlife.

TECHNICAL SUPPORT

Alex Acosta is a senior at Thomas Jefferson High School and has always been passionate about animals.

If you enjoyed this Sammy Puffin book,

please visit duaneziegler.com to learn about our other fun and educational books.

CHECK OUT THE JIMJIM SERIES!

The First Book In The JimJim Series

JimJim and his mouse family live near Sylvan Lake, high in the Rocky Mountains. JimJim and his brother and sisters must overcome the dangers of rainstorms, being lost, escaping Mr. Owl, dodging Rusty the Hawk, and dealing with Mr. Black Bear. Throughout their adventures is the chance to achieve greatness as a mouse and claiming their second name. Follow JimJim and his three siblings on their journey to survive the wilderness with the help of their new friends.

The Second Book In The JimJim Series

JimJim and his mouse family live near Sylvan Lake, high in the Rocky Mountains. Trapped in a backpack, the mice find themselves in Las Vegas. They have exciting times, but get swept outside into the street by accident. The mice are attacked by alley cats, visit many places in Vegas, learn new dances, make new friends, and learn karate. Follow JimJim and JoeJoe as they survive Vegas and find a way to return to Sylvan Lake with the help of their new friends.

The Third Book In The JimJim Series

JimJim and his mouse family live near Sylvan Lake, high in the Rocky Mountains. After a harrowing trip to Las Vegas, JimJim and his brother JoeJoe have returned home with their new friends Dr. Bruce and his assistants Haley and Danielle. Together, JimJim, his siblings, and their friends travel around Sylvan Lake helping animals in need. Follow JimJim and company on their adventures as they help the animals of Sylvan Lake and make new friends like Toby the Turtle, Sleepy the Mouse, Noah the Bunny, and Happy the Fawn!

Visit our website for new books, coloring books, and to meet the characters!

duaneziegler.com

CPSIA information can be obtained at www.ICGtesting.com
Printed in the USA
LVIW010748011219
638791LV00001BA/16